COOL
Relaxing

HEALTHY & FUN WAYS TO CHILL OUT

Alex Kuskowski

A Division of ABDO

ABDO
Publishing Company

visit us at www.abdopublishing.com

Published by ABDO Publishing Company, a division of ABDO, P.O. Box 398166, Minneapolis, Minnesota 55439. Copyright © 2013 by Abdo Consulting Group, Inc. International copyrights reserved in all countries. No part of this book may be reproduced in any form without written permission from the publisher. Checkerboard Library™ is a trademark and logo of ABDO Publishing Company.

Printed in the United States of America, North Mankato, Minnesota
062012
092012

 PRINTED ON RECYCLED PAPER

Design and Production: Mighty Media, Inc.
Series Editor: Liz Salzmann
Photo Credits: Colleen Dolphin, Shutterstock

The following manufacturers/names appearing in this book are trademarks: FabricMate®, HeatnBond®

Library of Congress Cataloging-in-Publication Data

Kuskowski, Alex.
  Cool relaxing : healthy & fun ways to chill out / Alex Kuskowski.
       p. cm. -- (Cool health & fitness)
  Includes index.
  ISBN 978-1-61783-428-8
  1. Relaxation--Juvenile literature. I. Title.
  RA785.K87 2012
  613.7'92--dc23
                                        2012010345

CONTENTS

CHILL OUT!

School. Soccer practice. Piano lessons. Homework. Hanging out with friends. Your life can get very busy! Sometimes that's overwhelming. One of the best things you can do for your body is to take time to relax.

Relaxing should be easy and fun. You'll feel better afterward too! That's why it's important to slow down for a few minutes every day. You'll have more energy later and you won't feel **stressed**. Take time to chill out. Find the best ways for you to unwind. Your mind and your body will thank you.

Permission & Safety

- Always get **permission** before doing these activities.
- Always ask if you can use the tools and supplies you need.
- If you do something by yourself, make sure you do it safely.
- Ask for help when necessary.
- Be careful when using sharp objects.
- Make sure you're wearing the **appropriate** gear.

Be Prepared

- Read the entire activity before you begin.
- Make sure you have all the tools and materials listed.
- Do you have enough time to complete the activity?
- Keep your work area clean and organized.
- Follow the directions.
- Clean up any mess you make.

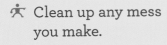

RELAX RIGHT

It takes some practice to get your relaxation **routine** just right. You have to find what works best for you. Try doing some breathing exercises. Take a long bath or go on a nature walk. Think of other ways to make your body and mind feel calm and **refreshed**. Remember to balance your life. It's an important part of being able to relax.

RELAXATION PREPARATION

> Write down what's bothering you to clear your mind.

> Avoid sugar and **caffeine**.

> Get a full night's sleep.

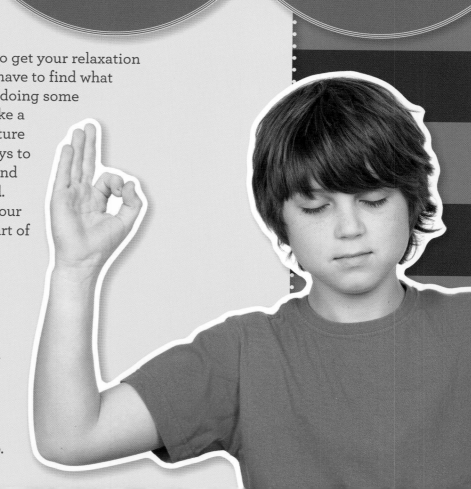

LET LOOSE

To relax you need to be prepared. You have to get rid of things that are on your mind in your daily life! It helps improve your relaxation time too. Here are five tips to start.

1. Manage your time. Make a list of everything you need to do in the day.

2. Leave time to relax. When you're feeling **stressed**, take a break.

3. Make goals. Work towards them.

4. Don't put too much on your daily list.

5. Practice! Everything takes practice, including relaxing.

MAKE TIME FOR BREAKS!

AROUND THE HOUSE (INSIDE)

There are tons of things you can do at home to relax. Get creative about it! Don't just sit in front of the TV. Find something calm to do that you enjoy.

LAUGH IT OFF

If you're feeling **stressed** and want to relax, try a laugh. Check out a joke book, or go online and look up funny stories. Tell them to your friends.

AROUND THE HOUSE (OUTSIDE)

If you have nice weather you can enjoy the fresh air outside. Try exercising outdoors to relax. Go for a run or fly a kite.

PLUGGED IN

Computers are used for a lot of things. Most kids use them for talking to friends and doing homework. You can use your computer to relax by making a playlist of your favorite music.

ON THE ROAD

Car rides, especially road trips, can seem like they take forever. Try practicing **meditation**. Before you know it, you'll arrive at your **destination**.

AT SCHOOL

Most of the day you don't get to choose what you're doing. Your brain can get tired from all the work. Take a break when you can and do some relaxing stretches.

WITH FRIENDS

When you're with your friends it's even easier to relax. Your friends are always there to make you feel less **stressed**. Try playing a favorite game together.

SETTLE DOWN CENTER

CALMING COOKIES

Make or bake a tasty dessert. You'll feel like you accomplished something even while you're relaxing. And you'll have a sweet treat!

FUN RUN

People with a lot of energy like to relax by working out. Try running, biking, or swimming. You'll feel great afterward!

SERENE READING

Grab a book! Read an old favorite or start something new. There's nothing more relaxing than curling up with a good book.

BUBBLY BATHS

Getting clean in a bubble bath can relax your whole body! Play with bath toys or just splash around.

SWEEP IT OUT!

Make sure your room is clean before you relax. Pick up your clothes or sweep the floor. You'll be surprised at how great it feels to be neat and organized!

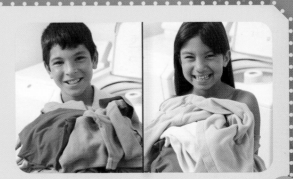

SUPPLIES

Here are some of the things that you'll need to get started!

dried lavender

dried rose petals

fabric

fabric markers
(optional)

fusible bonding tape

hair binders

iron

lemon juice

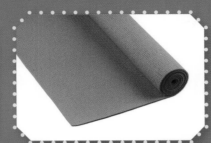

exercise mat

measuring tape

olive oil

paper

ribbon

round sticker

small jar with lid

rubber spatula

Perfect Poses

🏠 Energize with Yoga!

WHAT YOU NEED

- exercise mat

Tranquil Tree

1 Stand with your feet 12 inches (30 cm) apart. Press your hands together in front of your chest. Slowly lift your left foot off the ground.

2 Wait until you are well-balanced. Then press the bottom of your left foot to your right leg. See if you can balance for 30 seconds. Remember to keep your breathing slow.

3 Try switching feet. If you feel **confident** hold your arms up. Sway like a tree in the wind.

Downward Dog

4 Kneel on the mat. Put your hands about 12 inches (30 cm) in front of your knees. Keep your back flat.

5 Push up on your toes and your hands. Your arms and legs should be straight. From the side you will look like an upside down V. Lift up your left foot. After 10 seconds bring it down. Then try lifting up the other leg.

Child's Pose

6 Do this pose last. Kneel on the mat. Slowly bend forward until your head touches the mat. Stretch your arms out in front of you. Or lay your arms at your sides with your hands by your feet. Relax and breathe slowly. Hold this pose for 30 seconds.

Super Stretches

Easy stretches to relax your muscles!

WHAT YOU NEED

- exercise mat
- towel

Happening Hamstrings

1 Lie on your back on the mat. Lift your legs straight up in the air.

2 Throw the towel over the top of your feet. Hold both ends of the towel and pull down. Don't let your knees bend. You should feel a stretch in the back of your legs. Hold it for 10 seconds.

Arm Stretches

3 Stand on the mat. Hold one end of the towel with your right hand. Let the towel hang down your back. Grab the other end with your left hand. Pull with both arms for 10 seconds. Then switch arms and pull again for 10 seconds.

Side Stretches

4 Stand on the mat. Hold each end of the towel. Raise your arms straight up in the air.

5 Lean to the right as far as you can. Hold it for 10 seconds. Then lean to the left and hold it for 10 seconds. Repeat five times.

Luscious Lemon Scrub

 Time to pamper your face!

WHAT YOU NEED

- 1 cup sugar
- 2 tablespoons olive oil
- 4 tablespoons lemon juice
- mixing bowl
- rubber spatula
- measuring cup
- measuring spoon
- small jar with lid
- round sticker
- markers

1. Put the sugar, olive oil, and lemon juice in a mixing bowl. Mix well with a spatula.

2. Pour the mixture into a small jar. Put the lid on the jar.

3. Use markers and a sticker to make a fun label for the jar.

4. To use, scoop some out with your fingers. Scrub your face for 3 minutes. Then rinse with warm water. Pat your face dry with a towel.

TIP: After using the scrub smooth on your favorite lotion!

Lavender Pillow

 Breathe in and relax on the road with this pillow!

WHAT YOU NEED

- fabric, 16 × 24 inches (40 × 60 cm)
- measuring tape
- measuring cup
- scissors
- fusible bonding tape
- iron
- 2 hair binders
- marker
- ½ cup dried rose petals
- ½ cup dried lavender
- pillow stuffing
- 2 16-inch (40 cm) strips of ribbon
- fabric markers (optional)

1 Lay the fabric right side up. Cut a strip of bonding tape 24 inches (60 cm) long. Lay it on one of the long edges of the fabric. Make sure the paper side is facing up.

2 Have an adult help you use the iron. Iron the entire bonding strip for 1 to 2 seconds. Let it cool. Pull off the paper. There should be a sticky film left.

3 Fold the fabric. Line up the edges with the strip of tape between them. Have an adult help you run the iron over the seam. Let it cool.

4 Turn the fabric so the right side is facing out. Measure 4 inches (10 cm) in from one end of the tube. Wrap a hair binder tightly around that spot.

5 Put the pillow stuffing, rose petals, and lavender in the other end. When the tube is almost full, close the end with another hair binder. Tie ribbons over the hair binders to hide them. Then use the pillow to get a restful sleep on your trip!

TIP: Use fabric markers to make your pillow **unique**. Add your name or draw designs!

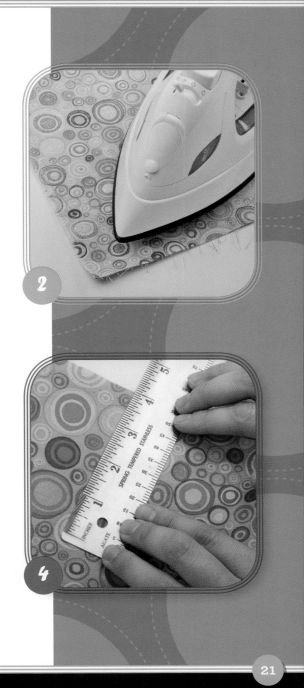

Computer Break

⏻ Stretch at your desk!

WHAT YOU NEED

- desk chair

Hand Fans

1 Stretch your arms out straight in front of you, and spread your fingers out as wide as you can. Hold for 10 seconds. Then relax and make a fist. Repeat ten times.

Shoulder Shrug

2 Lift your shoulders as close to your ears as you can. Then relax them as far away from your ears as they will go. Repeat ten times.

Wing Spread

3 Put your hands on the back of your head. Push your elbows back behind you. Hold it for three breaths. Repeat five times.

Torso Twist

4 Hold your elbows at your sides and don't move your hips or legs. Twist to look over your right shoulder. Then look over your left shoulder. Repeat five times.

Eyeball Figure Eights

5 Keep your head still. Move your eyes in figure eights. Look up to the right, down to the right, straight ahead, up to the left, down to the left and then straight ahead. Repeat five times.

Relax to the Max

Meditate to find inner calm!

meditating minds:

Try these tips to relax your breathing!

- Clear your head. Don't let your thoughts distract you.
- Breathe in through your nose and out through your mouth.
- Slow down your breathing.
- Give it a few minutes.
- Practice makes perfect.

WHAT YOU NEED

- just you

Beautiful Breathing

1 Find a quiet place you can sit. Rest your hands on your knees.

2 Close your eyes and listen to your breath.

3 Now imagine your favorite calm place to be. It could be on a beach or in the park.

Muscle Moves

4 Find a quiet place to sit. Take slow deep breaths.

5 When you are ready, scrunch up all the muscles in your face. Hold it for 10 seconds. Then relax.

6 Squeeze all the muscles in your neck and shoulders. Hold it for 10 seconds. Then relax.

7 Keep going down your body. Do the muscles in your stomach, arms, legs, and feet.

Lucky Labyrinth

Walk this way for relaxation!

WHAT YOU NEED

- pen
- paper
- large concrete area
- ruler
- chalk
- friends

1. Draw the design for the labyrinth on a piece of paper first. It could be **complicated** or just a **spiral**. If you want to make a traditional labyrinth follow the directions on pages 28 and 29.

2. Each path in your labyrinth should be 12 inches (30 cm) wide. Even if you make a spiral that only goes around twice that's a lot of space! Measure your concrete area to see if the labyrinth will fit.

3. Take your design outside and start drawing on the concrete with chalk. Measure often to make sure the path is wide enough.

4. When the labyrinth is finished admire your work! Now you can walk in it whenever you want. Or watch other people walk in it.

TIP: When you walk a labyrinth, do it slowly and calmly. Concentrate on the path and empty your mind of worries and **stresses**.

Ye Ol' Labyrinth

Make a labyrinth like the ancient Greeks!

WHAT YOU NEED

- pen
- paper
- large concrete area
- ruler
- chalk

1. Start by drawing a small cross. Then draw an angle in each section of the cross.

2. Add a dot on the outer corner of each section of the cross.

3. Connect the top of the cross to the line next to it on the right side. Use a small upside down U.

4. Move to the line to the left of the cross. Draw an arc connecting that to the dot on the right side.

5. Next draw a loop from the dot on the left, over the cross to the end of the top line on the right.

6. Keep moving around the cross, drawing more loops. Connect each dot or line on the left to the next dot or line on the right. Try to keep the paths evenly spaced.

7. The labyrinth is done when all the dots and lines are connected. There should be one opening at the bottom.

8. Use the directions on pages 26 and 27 to help draw your labyrinth outside. Make sure you have enough space!

Health Journal

Try keeping a health and fitness journal! Write about different ways you have tried to relax. Which ones worked? Did they take a long time? Were they easy to fit into your day? This makes it easy to look back and see how you are relaxing and reducing **stress**. It could also show you where there's room for improvement. Decorate your journal to show your personal style!

Glossary

appropriate – suitable, fitting, or proper for a specific occasion.

caffeine – a chemical in coffee, and some tea and soft drinks.

complicated – having many parts, details, ideas, or functions.

confident – sure of one's self and one's abilities.

destination – the place where you are going to.

meditation – the act of spending time in quiet thinking.

permission – when a person in charge says it's okay to do something.

refreshed – feeling full of new energy and strength.

routine – a regular order of actions or way of doing something.

spiral – a pattern that winds in a circle.

stress – mental or emotional strain or pressure.

unique – different, unusual, or special.

web sites

To learn more about health and fitness for kids, visit ABDO Publishing Company online at www.abdopublishing.com. Web sites about ways for kids to stay fit and healthy are featured on our Book Links page. These links are routinely monitored and updated to provide the most current information available.

Index